The Wizard of Oz

The Wizard of Oz

Retold by Freya Littledale

Illustrated by Myra Lowenthal

SCHOLASTIC BOOK SERVICES
NEW YORK · TORONTO · LONDON · AUCKLAND · SYDNEY · TOKYO

ISBN 0-590-31610-9

12 11 10 9 8 7 6 5 4 3 2   3 4 5 6 7/8

Printed in the U. S. A.   09

For Glenn

The Cyclone

On a small farm in the great Kansas prairies, there was once a young girl called Dorothy. She lived in a tiny house with her Aunt Em, Uncle Henry, and her dog Toto.

One afternoon Toto began to bark wildly. Dorothy heard the wind howl. She looked outside and saw the sky grow as dark as night.

"A cyclone is coming!" she cried. Quickly she took Toto in her arms.

Then a strange thing happened. The house whirled around three times in the wind. It rose high in the air and was carried away like a feather. Dorothy was very frightened.

Hours passed. The wind shrieked and the house swayed. Dorothy crawled into bed. "Everything will be all right," she told Toto over and over again. And soon she closed her eyes and fell asleep.

The Land of the Munchkins

When Dorothy woke up, the house was still. Sunshine filled the room. She ran outside with Toto and she could hardly believe her eyes. The cyclone had set the house down in a beautiful land. All around her were wonderful fruit trees. Brightly colored birds perched on the branches and flowers grew everywhere.

A little old woman and three little men came toward the house. They were no bigger than Dorothy. "Welcome to the Land of the Munchkins," said the little old woman. "We thank you for killing the Wicked Witch of the East."

"I don't understand," said Dorothy. "I never killed anyone."

"Your house did," said the little old woman, "and that is almost the same thing. It fell right on top of her. Look!"

Dorothy looked and saw two feet in silver shoes sticking out from under the house. "Oh, my!" she cried. The two feet began to fade away until nothing was left but the silver shoes.

"The Wicked Witch of the East is dead," said the little old woman. "Now the Munchkins are free."

"Who are the Munchkins?" asked Dorothy.

"The Munchkins are my friends," said the little old woman. The three strange little men took off their hats and bowed. "And *I* am the Good Witch of the North."

"I thought all witches were wicked," said Dorothy.

"Oh, no, dear child," said the little old woman. "Now that the Witch of the East is dead, there is only one wicked witch in the Land of Oz — the Wicked Witch of the West. She is very powerful indeed. But there are two good witches. I am one of them."

"Can you help me get back to my Aunt Em and Uncle Henry?" asked Dorothy.

"I will try," said the little old woman. "But first please take the silver shoes. I know they're magic shoes. But I don't know what they can do." Dorothy put on the shoes and they fitted her perfectly.

Then the little old woman took off her hat. She

held it on the tip of her nose and counted, "One . . . two . . . three!" At once the hat turned into a slate that said: SEND DOROTHY TO THE CITY OF EMERALDS.

"Aha!" said the little old woman. "I knew it! You must go to Emerald City and see the great Wizard of Oz. He can help you get back home."

Then the little old woman kissed Dorothy on her forehead. Her lips left a small, shining mark. "No harm can come to you now."

"Please tell me how I get to Emerald City," said Dorothy.

"Follow the yellow brick road," said the little old woman. Then she spun around on her heels and disappeared.

The Scarecrow, the Tin Woodman, and the Cowardly Lion

Dorothy set out at once with Toto right behind her. It wasn't long before she found the yellow brick road. She walked and walked until she came to a cornfield.

"Can you get me down?" called a voice.

Dorothy looked up and saw a Scarecrow hanging from a pole. "Did you speak?" asked Dorothy.

"Yes, I did," said the Scarecrow. "Can you please get me down from here? This pole is stuck up my back."

Dorothy reached up and took the Scarecrow off the pole. "Thank you very much," said the Scarecrow. "I might have done it myself if I had brains."

"Don't you have any brains?" asked Dorothy.

"No," said the Scarecrow sadly. "I'm stuffed with straw."

"That's too bad," said Dorothy. "Why don't you come with me to Emerald City? I'm going to ask the great Wizard of Oz to send me back to Kansas. You can ask him for brains."

"I'd like that very much," said the Scarecrow. And he and Dorothy went on their way with Toto right behind them.

Suddenly they heard a loud groan. "Ugh!" They turned and saw a Woodman holding up an ax. The Woodman was made of tin.

"Did you groan?" asked Dorothy.

"Yes," said the Tin Woodman. "I'm so rusty I can't move. Please get the oil can for me. It's in my hut behind those trees."

Dorothy ran to the hut and returned with the oil. Then she oiled the Woodman's arms and neck and legs.

The Tin Woodman put down his ax and moved his legs. "Oh, thank you!" he said. "Now if I only had a heart I'd be happy."

"Don't you have a heart?" asked Dorothy.

"No," said the Tin Woodman. "The Wicked Witch of the East turned me into tin and took away my heart."

"I'm sorry," said Dorothy. "Why don't you come with us to Emerald City? I'm going to ask the great Wizard of Oz to send me back to Kansas. The Scarecrow is going to ask him for brains. You can ask him for a heart."

"That would be wonderful!" said the Tin Woodman. And he and Dorothy and the Scarecrow went on their way with Toto right behind them.

All at once they heard a horrible roar. A great Lion leaped onto the road. He knocked down the Scarecrow with one blow of his paw. Then he struck the Tin Woodman with his sharp claws.

Toto barked loudly. The lion opened his mouth to bite the little dog. But Dorothy ran over and slapped the Lion on his nose.

"Don't you dare bite my dog!" she cried. "What's the matter with you? How can such a big Lion bite a little dog?"

"I didn't bite him," said the Lion.

"You tried to," said Dorothy. "You're nothing but a big coward!"

The Lion bowed his head. "I know it," he said. "The Lion should be King of the Beasts. But I'm not. I have no courage." And the Lion wiped a tear from his eye with the tip of his tail.

"Why don't you come with us to Emerald City?" said Dorothy. "I'm going to ask the great Wizard of Oz to send me back to Kansas. The Scarecrow is going to ask him for brains. The Tin Woodman is going to ask for a heart. Maybe you could ask him for courage."

"If you don't mind, I will," said the Lion. And off they went along the yellow brick road.

The Poppy Field

Soon they came to a field of beautiful red poppies. The smell of the flowers was very strong. Dorothy rubbed her eyes and yawned. "I'm so sleepy," she said. Then she lay down and closed her eyes.

"Get up!" cried the Tin Woodman. "The smell of these poppies is poisonous!" He tried pulling Dorothy to her feet. But she soon fell down again with Toto by her side.

"What are we going to do?" cried the Tin Woodman.

"If we leave her here she'll sleep forever," said the Lion. "I can hardly stay awake myself."

"Get out of this field as fast as you can," the Scarecrow told the Lion. "We'll take care of Dorothy. But you're too big to carry."

So the Lion ran ahead. The Scarecrow and the Tin Woodman made a chair with their hands and carried Dorothy and Toto. On and on they walked through the field of poppies. Soon they saw the Lion. He had fallen asleep among the flowers.

"Poor Lion," said the Tin Woodman. "He'll never wake up again."

"There's nothing we can do," said the Scarecrow. "We must go on."

It wasn't long before they reached the end of the poppy field. They laid Dorothy on the grass beside a river where she could breathe the fine fresh air.

The Field Mice

Suddenly they heard a deep growl. "GRRRRR!" They saw a big wildcat chasing a tiny field mouse. Quickly the Tin Woodman raised his ax and killed the wildcat.

"Oh, thank you!" said the field mouse. "You saved my life!"

"I like helping anyone in trouble," said the Tin Woodman, "even a mouse."

"Even a mouse!" cried the little animal. "Why *I* am Queen of all the field mice!" As she spoke, hundreds of mice came running. "Oh, Your Majesty," they cried, "we thought the wildcat killed you! How did you ever escape?"

"The Tin Woodman saved me," said the Queen. "Now you must do whatever he wishes."

"I wish you would help us save the Cowardly Lion," said the Scarecrow. "The Tin Woodman can build a cart. If each mouse brings a piece of string, we'll pull the Lion out of the poppy field."

And that is just what they did. The Tin Woodman built the cart. The mice brought the string. Then the mice were tied to the cart like a team of tiny horses.

They pulled it right to the poppy field and carried the sleeping Lion safely away.

"Thank you for saving our friend," said the Tin Woodman.

"Thank you for saving our Queen," said the mice. And they ran off to their homes in the field.

After a while Dorothy and the Lion woke up. Then they set out once more along the yellow brick road.

Emerald City

Soon they saw a green glow in the sky. The glow grew brighter and brighter as they came close to the gate of Emerald City. The gate was covered with emeralds that shone in the sunlight.

Dorothy rang the bell and a little man came to greet them. He was dressed in green from head to toe.

"We have come to see the great Wizard of Oz," said Dorothy. "We have something important to ask him."

"Very well," said the little man. "I am the Guardian of the Gates and I will take you to his palace. First you must put on glasses. Without them, the brightness of the city could blind you."

The Guardian of the Gates opened a big green box. He found green glasses for Dorothy, the Scarecrow, the Tin Woodman, and the Lion. He even put glasses on little Toto.

"Follow me," he told them.

Dorothy and her friends could hardly believe their eyes. The streets of the city were paved with green

marble and studded with emeralds. The people were dressed in green and had greenish skins. Children were buying green popcorn and green lemonade. Dorothy saw them pay with green coins.

They soon came to a palace in the middle of the city. A soldier with a long, green beard stood at the door. "Come in," said the soldier. "I will tell Oz you're here."

It was a long time before the soldier returned. "Did you see Oz?" asked Dorothy.

"No one ever sees Oz," said the soldier. "But I spoke to him behind his screen. He said he will meet one of you each day. Now you may go to your rooms and rest."

Then the soldier blew a whistle. At once a lovely girl with green hair bowed before Dorothy. She led her up three flights of stairs to a beautiful room. The bed was covered with green silk sheets and a velvet quilt. A tiny fountain shot sprays of green perfume into the air. The closet was filled with green dresses that were just the right size for Dorothy.

"Oz will see you in the morning," said the green girl. And she left Dorothy and led the others to their rooms.

The Great Oz

The next morning Dorothy put on one of the pretty green dresses. She tied a green ribbon around Toto's neck. Then off she went to the Throne Room to see the Wizard of Oz.

The throne stood in the center of a big round room that was covered with emeralds. In the middle of the throne was a huge Head without a body or arms or legs.

The big eyes stared at Dorothy. The giant mouth moved. A voice spoke. "I am Oz, the Great and Terrible. Who are you?"

"I am Dorothy, the Small and Meek. I have come to ask for your help."

"Where did you get those silver shoes?" asked the Head.

"I got them from the Wicked Witch of the East," said Dorothy. "My house fell on her and killed her."

"Hmm," said the Head. "What do you wish from me?"

"Please help me get back to Kansas," said Dorothy. "I want to be with my Aunt Em and Uncle Henry again."

"What will you do in return?" asked the Head.

"What must I do?" asked Dorothy.

"You must kill the Wicked Witch of the West," said the Head.

"I can't do that!" Dorothy cried. "I have never killed anyone in my life."

"You must!" said the Head. "You have the silver shoes and you will find a way. Now go, and do not come back until the Wicked Witch is dead."

Dorothy left the Throne Room and told her friends what happened. "There's no hope!" she said. "I'll never see my Aunt Em or Uncle Henry again." Then she went back to her room and cried herself to sleep.

The next morning the Scarecrow entered the Throne Room. But he did not see a huge Head. He saw a lovely Lady with wings.

"I am Oz, the Great and Terrible. Who are you?" asked the Lady.

"I am a Scarecrow stuffed with straw. I have come to ask you for brains."

"If you help Dorothy kill the Wicked Witch of the West, I will give you brains," said the Lady.

The following morning the Tin Woodman went to the Throne Room. He did not see a huge Head or a lovely Lady. He saw a horrible Beast with five arms and five legs.

"I am Oz, the Great and Terrible," roared the Beast. "Who are you?"

"I am a Woodman made of tin. I have come to ask for a heart."

"When the Wicked Witch of the West is dead, I will give you a heart," said the Beast. "Now go!"

The next morning the Lion went to the Throne Room. He did not see a huge Head, a lovely Lady, or a horrible Beast. He saw a great Ball of Fire.

"I am Oz, the Great and Terrible," said the Ball of Fire. "Who are you?"

"I am the Cowardly Lion. I have come to ask you for courage."

"Bring me proof that the Wicked Witch is dead," said the Ball of Fire. "Then I will give you courage. Otherwise, you will remain a coward forever."

The Lion was angry at these words. But the Ball of Fire grew so hot, he ran from the room. He was glad to see his friends waiting for him.

"What are we going to do?" asked Dorothy.

"There is only one thing we can do," said the Lion. "We must kill the Wicked Witch of the West."

The Wicked Witch

The next morning Dorothy and her friends left Emerald City. The Guardian of the Gates took off their glasses and unlocked the gate.

"Where can we find the Wicked Witch of the West?" asked Dorothy.

"She lives in the Country of the Winkies," he answered. "Keep to the West, where the sun sets, and you will find her."

Dorothy and her friends walked and walked. The ground was rough and hilly. There were no trees to shade them from the hot sun. Before dark, Dorothy, Toto, and the Lion lay down on the grass to rest. The Tin Woodman and the Scarecrow watched over them.

Meanwhile, the Wicked Witch stood at the door of her castle. The Witch had only one eye. But that eye was so powerful, she could see everything for miles around.

When the Witch saw Dorothy and her friends, she ran to her cupboard and grabbed a Golden Cap. Now, this Cap had magic powers. Whoever wore it could command the Winged Monkeys three times. They had to obey. The Witch had used it twice before. This was her last command.

She stood on her left foot and said, "Ep-pe, pep-pe, kak-ke!"

She stood on her right foot and said, "Hil-lo, hol-lo, hel-lo!"

Then she stood on both feet and cried, "Ziz-zy, zuz-zy, zik!"

The sky grew dark and a low rumble filled the air. Down to the Witch's castle flew a crowd of Monkeys with powerful wings. "You have called us for the third and last time," said the leader. "What is your command?"

"Go to those strangers and kill them!" said the Witch. "But bring the Lion back alive. I will harness him like a horse and make him work."

The Winged Monkeys flew away. In an instant, they lifted the Tin Woodman way up in the air and dropped him over sharp rocks.

They pulled every bit of straw from the Scarecrow. Then they threw his clothes high on a treetop.

They tied up the Lion with strong rope and carried him back to the castle yard.

After this, the leader of the Monkeys flew over to Dorothy. She clung tightly to Toto. She was so frightened she could hear the beating of her own heart. The Monkey grinned a terrible grin and reached out to grab her. Then he stopped when he saw the shining mark on her forehead. "We cannot hurt this child," he told the other monkeys. "She is protected by the kiss of the Good Witch. All we can do is take her to the castle."

So they lifted Dorothy, with Toto in her arms, and carried her back to the Witch.

"You have used your last wish," the leader told the Witch. "You will never see us again." Then the Winged Monkeys flew up in the air and were gone.

At the Witch's Castle

The Wicked Witch was surprised to see the mark on Dorothy's forehead. She knew that she dare not hurt her. But when she saw the silver shoes, she thought, "Aha, the magic shoes! I will soon have them for myself."

Then the Witch went to the yard to harness the Cowardly Lion. The Lion roared and opened his mouth to bite her. The Witch was so frightened, she ran out and locked the gate behind her.

"If I can't harness you, I will starve you to death," said the Witch. "You will get no food until you do what I want."

Every day she went to the gate and asked the Lion, "Are you ready for the harness?"

And every day the Lion answered, "No! If you come near me, I will bite you."

But at night, while the Witch was asleep, Dorothy took food to the Lion. After he had eaten, she would rest her head on his shaggy mane and talk about escaping. There seemed no way out. The castle was guarded night and day by the Winkies. The Witch had made slaves of them all and they had to obey her.

Now the Witch wanted Dorothy's shoes more than anything in the world. At last she thought of a plan. One morning, while Dorothy was washing the kitchen floor, the Witch tripped her with an iron bar. As Dorothy fell, one silver shoe came off. Quickly the Witch grabbed the shoe and put it on.

"Give me back my shoe!" cried Dorothy.

"I will not!" said the Witch. "This shoe is mine. I'll get the other one, too! Wait and see!"

Dorothy was very angry. She picked up a pail of water and threw it over the Witch. "You wicked thing!" she cried.

"Ahhhhhhhh!" screamed the Witch. "Look what you've done!"

Dorothy looked in wonder as the Witch began to melt before her eyes.

"Didn't you know water would be the end of me?" sobbed the Witch.

"How could I?" asked Dorothy.

"Oh! Oh!" cried the Witch. "Here I goooooo!" With these words she melted completely away.

Dorothy picked up the silver shoe and ran outside. "We're free!" she told the Lion. "I melted the Witch with a pail of water!"

"We're all free!" she called to the Winkies. "The Wicked Witch is dead!"

"Hurray!" they shouted. And everyone sang and danced.

"If only the Scarecrow and the Tin Woodman were here," said the Lion.

The Rescue

"We'll help you rescue them," said the Winkies. And they set out the very next morning. It wasn't long before they found the Tin Woodman. He was all battered and bent. The Winkies carried him back to the castle where the tinsmiths worked for three days and nights. They hammered and pounded and polished until the Tin Woodman was as good as new.

Next they went in search of the Scarecrow. They found his clothes on the treetop where the Monkeys had dropped them. The Tin Woodman chopped down the tree with his ax. Then the Winkies carried the clothes back to the castle and stuffed them with nice clean straw. The Scarecrow looked better than ever.

At last they were all together again. Dorothy and her friends spent many happy days with the Winkies. The Winkies liked the Tin Woodman so much, they asked him to be their ruler.

"I cannot rule without a heart," said the Woodman.

"We must go back to the Wizard of Oz."

"Yes," said the Scarecrow. "I want my brains."

"I want my courage," said the Lion.

"And I want to go home to Kansas," said Dorothy.

So they thanked the Winkies and said good-bye.

When Dorothy went to the kitchen to get food for the journey, she saw the Golden Cap. She did not know it was a magic Cap. But she thought it was pretty, so she took it along.

Then Dorothy and her friends went back to the Wizard's palace. The soldier with the long, green beard let them in at once.

The Discovery

Dorothy and her friends entered the Throne Room together. They heard nothing. They saw no one. After a while a voice spoke. "I am Oz, the Great and Terrible."

They looked around them. Still they saw no one. "Where are you?" asked Dorothy.

"I am everywhere," said the voice. "What are you doing here?"

"You promised to send me home to Kansas when the Wicked Witch was dead," said Dorothy.

"You promised me brains," said the Scarecrow.

"You promised me a heart," said the Tin Woodman.

"You promised me courage," said the Lion.

"Is the Witch really dead?" asked the voice.

"Yes," said Dorothy. "I melted her with a pail of water."

"My, oh my!" said the voice. "Well, come back tomorrow. I need time to think."

"You've had enough time," said the Scarecrow.

"We won't wait," said the Tin Woodman.

"You must keep your promise!" cried Dorothy.

The Lion said nothing. He just roared loudly. "GRRRRRRRR!" The roar surprised Toto. He jumped away and tipped over a screen in the corner. All of them stared in wonder.

There stood a little old man with a bald head and wrinkled face.

"Who are you?" asked the Tin Woodman.

"I am Oz, the Great and Terrible," whispered the little old man.

"I thought Oz was a huge Head," said Dorothy.

"I thought Oz was a lovely Lady," said the Scarecrow.

"I thought Oz was a horrible Beast," said the Tin Woodman.

"I thought Oz was a Ball of Fire," said the Lion.

"You are all wrong," said the little old man. "That was just make-believe."

"Make-believe!" cried Dorothy. "Aren't you a great Wizard?"

"No, my dear, I'm just a common man. Come. I will show you some of my tricks."

He led them into a back room. In one corner was the huge Head. It was made out of paper with a face painted on it. The lovely Lady was just a mask. The horrible Beast was nothing but skins sewn together.

The Ball of Fire was a big ball of cotton that hung from the ceiling. When oil was poured on it, the ball burned wildly.

"What about the voice?" asked Dorothy.

"I am a ventriloquist," said the little old man. "I can make my voice sound like it's coming from anywhere."

"You are a humbug!" said the Scarecrow.

"That is true," said the little old man. "I am a humbug. But I couldn't help it. Listen and I will tell you my story.

"When I was a young man, I was a balloonist with a circus. One day my balloon went way up in the air and floated far away to this beautiful country. The people saw me coming down from the sky. They thought I was a great Wizard and promised to do anything I wished.

"So I asked them to build Emerald City. Then I had green glasses put on all the people so everything they saw looked green."

"But everything *is* green — even the popcorn," said Dorothy.

"No," said Oz. "The green glasses make it seem that way. Still, this is a beautiful city and the people are happy. I've been good to them and they like me. But the Wicked Witches would have destroyed me if they had known I wasn't a Wizard. They really had magic powers. I have none. That is why I can't keep my promises to you."

"I think you're a bad man," said Dorothy.

"No, I'm a very good man. But I am a bad Wizard."

"Maybe you are," said the Scarecrow. "But I still want my brains."

"I still want my heart," said the Tin Woodman.

"And I want my courage," said the Lion.

"All right," said Oz. "Come to me tomorrow and you will all have what you want. I've been a make-believe Wizard for so long, one day more won't matter."

"What about me?" asked Dorothy. "How will I get home to Kansas?"

"I'll try to think of something," said Oz. "But please don't tell anyone I'm a humbug."

"We won't," they promised.

The Humbug's Magic

The next morning the Scarecrow went to see Oz. "I have come for my brains," he said.

"They're right here," said Oz. Then he took off the Scarecrow's head and filled it with bran mixed with pins and needles. "Now you have bran-new brains," said Oz as he put the head back on.

The Scarecrow could hardly wait to see his friends. "I feel so wise!" he told them.

"Why are those pins and needles sticking out of your head?" asked the Tin Woodman.

"They prove he's sharp," said the Lion.

"Well, it's my turn now," said the Tin Woodman.

And he went to the Throne Room. "I have come for my heart," he said.

"I must cut a hole so I can put your heart in the right place," said Oz.

"I don't mind," said the Tin Woodman.

Oz cut the tin very carefully. He gave the Tin Woodman a fine silk heart.

"How can I ever thank you?" said the Tin Woodman.

"It was nothing," said Oz.

The Lion was next. He went to the Throne Room and said, "I have come for my courage."

"It's ready," said Oz. And he placed a beautiful bowl before the Lion. "Drink," he said.

The Lion sniffed. "What's in the bowl?" he asked. "It looks like green water."

"Never mind," said Oz. "When it's inside you, it will be courage."

The Lion drank quickly. "Ah!" he said. "At last I feel full of courage!" And he went proudly back to his friends.

The Great Balloon

A few days later Oz sent for Dorothy. "I have a plan," he told her. "Let's make a balloon and we'll both fly to Kansas."

"Do you want to go, too?" asked Dorothy.

"Yes," said Oz. "I'm tired of being a humbug."

So they set to work with needle and thread and a big bag of green silk. They sewed and sewed until the balloon was finished.

The great day came. The balloon was carried in front of the palace where everyone was waiting. Oz stepped inside the basket and spoke to the people. "While I am away, the wise Scarecrow will rule Emerald City. You must all obey him."

"Now hurry, Dorothy," he called, "or the balloon will fly away without you."

Dorothy was chasing Toto who was running after a cat. "Hurry!" Oz called again.

At last she caught Toto and ran toward the balloon. "Wait for me!" Dorothy shouted. But it was too late. The ropes broke, and the balloon was rising to the sky. "Come back!" cried Dorothy.

"I can't," he called. "Good-bye!"

"Good-bye!" the people shouted. And that was the last they saw of the wonderful Wizard of Oz.

Dorothy's eyes filled with tears. "How am I ever going to get back home!" she cried.

"Don't worry," said the Scarecrow. "I will think of something." And he sent for the soldier with the green beard.

"Glinda will help," said the soldier. "She is the Good Witch of the South.

On the Road to the South

The very next morning Dorothy and her friends set out on the road to the South. The Scarecrow led the way. They walked and walked until they reached a deep dark forest.

"Ooooo, what a gloomy place!" the Scarecrow said.

"I think it's beautiful!" said the Lion.

Just as he spoke, he saw hundreds of animals holding a meeting. A huge tiger ran up to him and said, "Welcome, O King of Beasts. You have come just in time."

"What's wrong?" asked the Lion.

"A monster spider is in our forest," said the tiger. "It has killed many of us already. We'll all die if we don't kill the monster."

"Tell me," said the Lion, "are there any other lions in this forest?"

"There were," said the tiger, "but the monster ate them all."

"If I kill the monster, will you make me King of the Forest?" asked the Lion.

"Gladly!" said the tiger.

"Where is the monster now?" asked the Lion.

"Near the oak trees," said the tiger.

"I will go at once," said the Lion. And away he went.

There, fast asleep, was the ugliest spider he had ever seen. Its body was as big as an elephant. Its eight legs were as long as tree trunks. Only the neck was skinny. The Lion sprang on the monster's back. With one blow of his paw he knocked off the spider's head. Then he went back to the others.

"I have killed the monster spider," he told them.

All the animals bowed. "Thank you, Your Majesty."

"I must go with Dorothy now," said the Lion. "But I want to return very soon."

The Good Witch of the South

At last Dorothy and her friends reached Glinda's castle. The Good Witch Glinda sat on a ruby throne. Her hair was long and red, and her eyes were like blue jewels.

"What can I do for you?" she asked.

Dorothy told the Witch her story. Then she said, "All I want now is to go home to Kansas and be with my Aunt Em and Uncle Henry again."

"I will help you, dear child," said Glinda. "First you must give me the Golden Cap."

Then the Witch asked the Scarecrow, "What will you do when Dorothy leaves?"

"I would like to go back to Emerald City," said the Scarecrow. "Oz made me its ruler."

"With this Golden Cap," said Glinda, "I will command the Winged Monkeys to carry you back to Emerald City."

"What will you do?" she asked the Tin Woodman.

"I want to return to the Winkies who asked me to be their ruler," said the Tin Woodman.

"With this Golden Cap," said Glinda, "I will command the Winged Monkeys to carry you to the Country of the Winkies."

Then the Witch looked at the Lion. "What will become of you when Dorothy leaves?"

"I want to go back to the forest where the animals made me King," said the Lion.

"My third and last command to the Winged Monkeys will be to carry you back to the forest," said Glinda.

"What about me?" asked Dorothy. "How will I get home to Kansas?"

"Your silver shoes will carry you there," said Glinda. "They had the power to take you back all along."

"If Dorothy had gone back, I would not have my brains," said the Scarecrow.

"I would not have my heart," said the Tin Woodman.

"And I would still be a coward," said the Lion.

"I'm glad you all have what you want most," said Dorothy. "But now I want to go home."

"Just click the heels of your silver shoes three times," said Glinda. "Tell them your wish and they'll carry you home in the wink of an eye."

"That's wonderful!" said Dorothy. "I'll ask them to take me back right now."

Then Dorothy kissed the Lion, the Tin Woodman, and the Scarecrow good-bye. She took Toto in her arms and clicked her heels three times. "Take me home to Kansas," she said.

Home at Last

At once Dorothy went spinning through the air. Then she came to a sudden stop and rolled over on the grass. Her silver shoes had fallen off in the flight and were gone forever.

"Oh, my!" Dorothy cried. Right in front of her eyes was a new farmhouse. Uncle Henry was milking the cows in the barn. Aunt Em was just coming out to water the cabbages.

Toto jumped from Dorothy's arms and barked happily. Aunt Em came running toward her. "My darling child!" she cried. "Where have you been?"

"In the Land of Oz," said Dorothy. "And oh, Aunt Em, I'm so glad to be home again!"